Jay Jay's Christmas Adventure

Adapted by Kirsten Larsen

Based on a teleplay by John Semper, Jr.

PSS!

PRICE STERN SLOAN

'Twas the night before Christmas, and Jay Jay, Tracy, and Snuffy were very excited. They were waiting for Santa Claus to arrive!

"Jay Jay, do you think Santa will like the Christmas tree I picked out?" Snuffy asked.

"I'm sure he will," Jay Jay replied. "See how beautiful it looks?" Indeed, with its colorful ornaments and lights, Snuffy's Christmas tree was the prettiest any of the young planes had ever seen.

"How do I look?" Tracy asked. "I want to look my best for Santa."

Jay Jay looked at her freshly polished wings and smiled. "You look great, Tracy," he said.

"Yeah, great!" Snuffy chimed in with a happy spin of his propeller.

Just then, Herky the Helicopter buzzed over to them.
"Guess what!" he shouted. "I was just at Brenda Blue's
workshop, and she heard on the radio that it is going
to snow."

"Snow!" Jay Jay and his friends cheered. A nice snowfall was just what they needed to make this the best Christmas Eve ever!

But instead of a nice light snowfall, what arrived that Christmas Eve was a big, windy snow*storm!*

"This is terrible," Tracy moaned. She and Snuffy had planned to stay up all night so they could meet Santa Claus. But now it looked like Santa might never arrive.

Jay Jay was worried, too. "I think I waited too long to send my Christmas wish list to Santa," he said. "With this storm, my list will never get to him."

Snuffy sniffled and his eyes filled with tears. "Look at my poor Christmas tree," he said. Snuffy's tree was so covered in snow that even the twinkling lights had lost their shine.

As Jay Jay, Tracy, and Snuffy stared out at the deepening piles of snow, Savannah landed on the runway. "Well, I do declare, I have never seen anything like this!" she exclaimed. "Sad children on Christmas Eve?"

"Our Christmas Eve is ruined," Jay Jay told her. "Look at all that snow!"

But Savannah just smiled. "Why Jay Jay, snow can't ruin Christmas Eve," she replied.

The three little planes looked at her in surprise. "Really?" asked Jay Jay.

"When it snows outside, you just hug the one next to you and do something nice and cheery to make yourself feel warm and happy inside," Savannah explained.

"Like what?" asked Tracy.

"Like sing a Christmas carol!" Savannah said.

All the planes thought that was a wonderful idea.
So they snuggled together and sang a Christmas song.

In no time at all, they were feeling warm and happy inside, just like Savannah said they would.

Meanwhile, over at Brenda Blue's workshop, an
emergency message had just come in for Old Oscar.
"At first I couldn't believe it," Brenda told the old
plane. "But then he said his name and . . . well, listen
for yourself." She flipped a switch on her radio so Old
Oscar could hear the message.

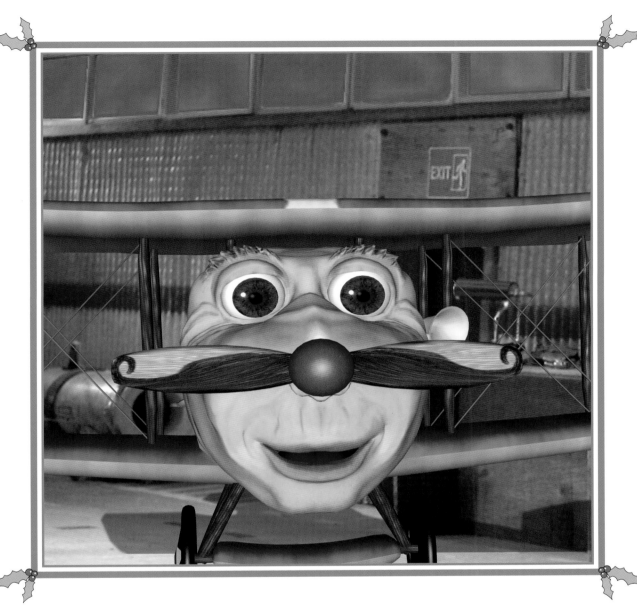

"This is Santa Claus," said a jolly voice. "I repeat, this is Santa Claus. I must speak to Oscar at Tarrytown Airport."

Old Oscar's eyes opened wide with surprise. "By golly, I'd recognize that voice anywhere," he cried. "Hey there, Santa Claus. It's me! Oscar!"

"Oscar, I need your help," said Santa. "One of my reindeer is sick, and I can't make all my Christmas deliveries. I was wondering if you and the planes at Tarrytown Airport might help me tonight."

"Why, sure we could," Oscar replied. "Except there's a snowstorm and we're all grounded."

"Ho, ho, ho," Santa laughed merrily. "That's no problem. I'll just call my friend Jack Frost and have that blizzard turned off."

True to his word, Santa arranged for the snowstorm to stop! Then the planes at Tarrytown Airport took off for the North Pole.

They flew a long, long way. At last Old Oscar said, "Look! There it is!"

Up ahead, at the very tip of the North Pole, they saw Santa's Workshop!

This was where Santa made all his toys.

Just as the planes landed, Santa came out the front door. "Well, if it isn't my old friend Oscar!" he cried. "How are you, my boy?"

"Oh, I'm just fine," said Old Oscar. "And I brought a few friends to meet you."

Jay Jay, Tracy, Snuffy, and Herky introduced themselves. "We're sorry about your sick reindeer, Santa," said Tracy. "But I'm happy to finally meet you!"

"Me too, Santa!" Herky piped up.

"I'm glad to be giving you what you want for Christmas, Tracy and Herky," Santa replied. "And Jay Jay, I *did* get your wish list. But send it a little earlier next time, okay?"

Jay Jay giggled. "Okay, Santa," he said.

"And Snuffy," Santa added, "I saw that beautiful Christmas tree you picked out. You did a very nice job." Santa smiled at all the planes. "Thank you all for being very special helpers tonight. Are you ready?"

"Ready!" the planes exclaimed, and they took off into the starry sky.

Jay Jay, Tracy, Snuffy, Herky, and Old Oscar spent the night delivering Santa's special toys to boys and girls all around the world.

After all the presents had been delivered, the planes
returned home to Tarrytown Airport. They were tired
but very happy. And what do you know—there, under
Snuffy's Christmas tree, was a big pile of presents!

"I was so busy having fun delivering presents that I forgot all about getting one myself!" said Jay Jay.

"I guess it was more fun giving Santa our help than getting presents from him," Tracy agreed.

"There's just one thing, though," Jay Jay said thoughtfully. "If we delivered all the presents to Tarrytown, then who delivered *our* presents?"

"Whoooooooaaaaaa!" someone overhead cried. All the planes looked up. It was Revvin' Evan, the fire engine. He was attached to a big hot air balloon!

"Looks like I got those gifts to you just in time!" he called to his friends. "It sure was fun helping Santa Claus. But there's only one teeny-tiny, eentsy-weentsy problem."

"What?" asked Jay Jay.

"You gotta get me down from here!" Evan shouted.
"Whooooooooaaaaaa!"

Well, they did manage to get Revvin' Evan down. Then they had the best Christmas Day ever. Full of fun, friendship, and giving, it was a Christmas they'd never forget!

"What?" asked Jay Jay.

"You gotta get me down from here!" Evan shouted. "Whooooooooaaaaaa!"

Well, they did manage to get Revvin' Evan down.
Then they had the best Christmas Day ever. Full of fun,
friendship, and giving, it was a Christmas they'd never
forget!